"I pretended to be somebody I wanted to be until finally, I became that person. Or he became me."

~ Cary Grant

Published by Herman Global Ventures 2020

My Super Me
Text Copyright © 2020 Todd Herman
Illustrations Copyright © 2020 Todd Herman

All inquiries should be directed to
www.ToddHerman.me

ISBN-13: 978-0-578-61244-7 Hardcover
ISBN-13: 978-0-578-62047-3 Paperback

To Molly, Sophie, & Charlie
and all the SuperKids...
The power inside is always stronger
than the force out there.

~TH

To Caen & Liav,
who inspire me every single day.

~ EJ

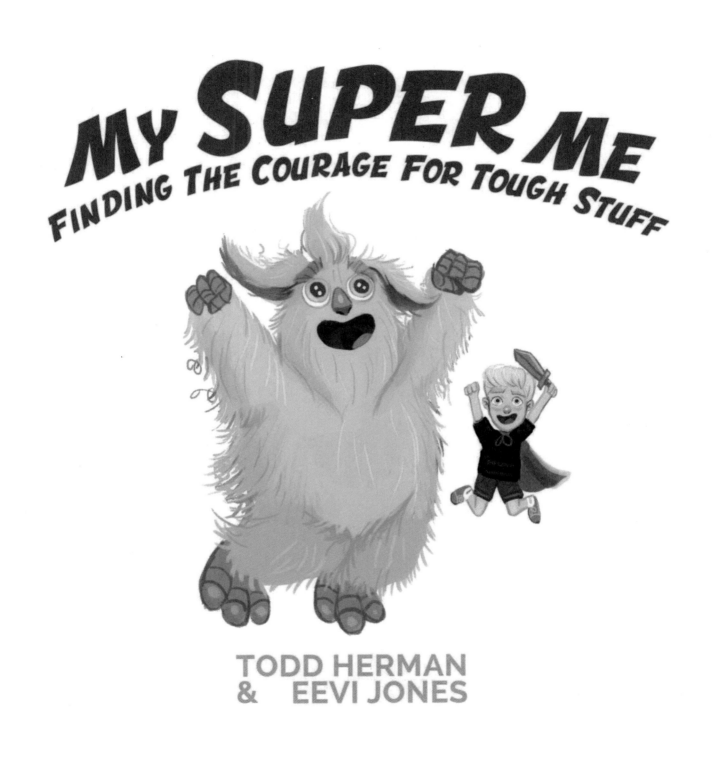

My SUPER Me
FINDING THE COURAGE FOR TOUGH STUFF

TODD HERMAN
&   EEVI JONES

SOMETIMES, THINGS ARE **HARD**.
SOMETIMES, THINGS ARE **TOUGH**.
SOMETIMES, WE **TRY** AND WE TRY
- AND IT'S STILL NOT **ENOUGH**.

THINGS ARE **HEAVY**, THEY'RE SCARY,
THEY'RE NEW, THEY'RE **OLD**.
THINGS ARE TOO **HARD**, TOO LOUD,
TOO HOT, OR TOO **COLD**.

When things are TOO something,
TOO this, or TOO that,
I may get quite ANGRY,
UPSET, or just SAD.

BUT **THEN** I REMEMBER THAT I'M **NEVER** ALONE. I REMEMBER MY **POWER** THAT'S **MIGHTY** AND STRONG.

A POWER SO **POWERFUL,**
IT **DOESN'T** KNOW FEAR.
A POWER SO **MIGHTY,**
INSIDE ME – RIGHT HERE!

He **LAUGHS** at the hard,
He laughs at the **TOUGH.**
He **LAUGHS** at a challenge
That's **THORNY** and rough.

I gave him a NAME, for a name gives HIM might. This name gives him POWER to FIGHT all my fights.

TO FIGHT ALL MY **BATTLES**,
MY **FEARS**, AND MY **SADS**.
TO FIGHT ALL MY **ANGRIES**,
MY **HURTS**, AND MY **BADS**.

I summon his POWERS. He QUICKLY transforms. He's the wind. He's the FORCE. He's CAPTAIN STORM!

A STORM THAT **LOVES** CHALLENGES,
BOTH **BIG** AND **SMALL.**
MY **FEARS** AND MY TOUGHS,
HE CONQUERS THEM **ALL.**

Forever CREATIVE,
PLAYFUL, AND STRONG.
EMBRACING EACH CHALLENGE,
HE SHOUTS,
"BRING IT ON!"

BRING IT ON, OH YOU **TROUBLE!**

BRING IT ON, OH YOU **FEAR!**

BRING IT ON, OH YOU **DOUBT,**

CUZ I AM **RIGHT** HERE!

I SUMMON MY **POWERS.**
I QUICKLY **TRANSFORM.**
I'M THE WIND! **I'M** THE FORCE!
I'M **CAPTAIN STORM!**

For **I AM** the brave one.
I show **COURAGE** galore.
Stepping into my **POWER**,
Stepping into my **MORE**.

I CAN **CHOOSE** HOW I ANSWER.
I CAN **CHOOSE** WHAT I FEEL.
I CAN **CHOOSE** WHAT I THINK,
WHAT I SAY, HOW I **DEAL.**

FOR IT'S UP TO ME
WHAT I CHOOSE TO BELIEVE,
AND KNOW MY HEROIC SELF
IS A PART OF ME.

WITH MY CAPE **AND** MY COURAGE
I NOW **CONQUER** MY FEAR.
FOR CAPTAIN STORM WAS **ME**
ALL ALONG,
ME –**RIGHT IN HERE.**

THE END

ABOUT THE AUTHORS

Todd Herman likes to activate the hero in everyone. He's an award-winning entrepreneur, WSJ bestselling author of *The Alter Ego Effect*, and creates training systems to develop peak performance & mental toughness for elite athletes, leaders, & public figures. He's busy building a movement from New York City where he lives with his wife and three children.

Check out his free resources at his home base on the internet – www.ToddHerman.me.

Eevi Jones is an award-winning and bestselling children's book author.

She lives near D.C. with her husband and their two boys.

She can be found at www.EeviJones.com.

OTHER BOOKS BY TODD HERMAN

An award-winning performance coach reveals the secret behind many top athletes and executives: creating a heroic Alter Ego to activate when the chips are down.

There's only one person in the way of you untapping all your capabilities: you. And you're also gifted with creative forces in your mind that can help reveal those capabilities, so you can remove the barriers of doubt, worry, and fear. That creative force is an Alter Ego and it just so happens to leverage the natural psychological wonders that make humans truly powerful.

The Alter Ego Effect unpacks the science of why this works, why & how you've already used this idea in some form, examples from people in sports, business, entertainment and every-day life, that have used this powerful concept. And the entire process for how to create one that allows you to tackle life with more grit and grace.

ATTENTION PARENTS

For more resources, including videos, downloads, and the *'Four Questions to Ask Kids at Bedtime'* to help develop your son or daughter's resilience, toughness, and confidence, go to: *www.mysuper.me*.

Made in the USA
San Bernardino, CA
10 June 2020